CLOWN

Blake

RED FOX

for Christine

A Red Fox Book
Published by Random House Children's Publishers UK
61-63 Uxbridge Road, London W5 5SA

A division of The Random House Group Ltd
Addresses for companies within The Random
House Group Limited can be found at:
www.randomhouse.co.uk/offices.htm

17 19 20 18

First published in Great Britain by Jonathan Cape 1995
Red Fox edition 1998

Printed in China

THE RANDOM HOUSE GROUP Limited Reg. No. 954009

ISBN 9780099493617

www.randomhousechildrens.co.uk